The
ENCHANTING LEGENDS OF
Shiloh Mansion

D. K. Ogans

The
ENCHANTING LEGENDS OF
Shiloh Mansion

the young king

TATE PUBLISHING
AND ENTERPRISES, LLC

Published by Tate Publishing & Enterprises, LLC

127 E. Trade Center Terrace | Mustang, Oklahoma 73064 USA
1.888.361.9473 | www.tatepublishing.com

Tate Publishing is committed to excellence in the publishing industry. The company reflects the philosophy established by the founders, based on Psalm 68:11,

"The Lord gave the word and great was the company of those who published it."

Book design copyright © 2013 by Tate Publishing, LLC. All rights reserved.
Cover design by Allen Jomoc
Interior design by Honeylette Pino

Published in the United States of America

ISBN: 978-1-62854-350-6
1. Fiction / Christian / Fantasy
2. Fiction / Action & Adventure
13.07.26

DEDICATION

First, I want to thank the Lord, "the Great I Am," who is the master teacher, for impressing upon my heart a desire to share that he truly does make a difference in our lives! He has given me a heart of a child who eagerly desires to share the truth of his Word! His omnipotent power supersedes any other power or principality! We all can benefit greatly from the biblical principles found in the Scriptures once we begin to actually embrace them within our own lives!

The Enchanting Legends is dedicated with love to my dear husband/pastor and best friend, Randall Ogans Sr.; our adult children—Nicole Elyse, Randall II, Jamal, Julian, and Dorian; their spouses; and all of their children, our dear grandchildren! In the eyes of God, we are all children! I pray that this is enjoyed by everyone who is bravely delighted and interested into delving deeper into the thrilling meaning of life—the young, old, and everyone in between anywhere and everywhere throughout the world!

INTRODUCTION

The Enchanting Legends of Shiloh Mansion is written in a simplistic fashion where any and every one can enjoy the great legends of the Bible, the Book of I Am! Here, within *The Enchanting Legends of Shiloh Mansion*, one can become familiar with the true source of ultimate power, the most awesome, extraordinary, luminous universal power, our Creator and Maker, the Great I Am, the God Most High! One can discover the magnificent love story between God and mankind and the wonderful intriguing truth found in his marvelous Book of I Am where there really are authentic superheroes!

Learning can be marvelously exhilarating fun! Reading can take us on a plethora of amazing, astounding fabulous journeys! It is a passageway into the past, present, and future! It does not have to be a dreadful, tedious, grueling experience! There is a wealth of wisdom just waiting to open our understanding and help us live well-rounded, fulfilling lives! An exciting life of continual spiritual growth and discovery awaits us! Please, if you will step into a marvelous dimension of meaningful living with a purpose, your life can become transformed; and you shall receive power!

You will see that you are here on earth for a reason. Come and experience a spectacular awe-inspiring journey with me into a land where the timeless historical truths of the Book of I Am are revisited. Here, you will also meet an intriguing, beautiful, wonderfully fascinating, make-believe mythical family of characters with remarkable abilities, talents, and gifts that share their journeys. Their faith is activated, all because they truly believe in the Great I Am! Although the characters are imaginary, the principles they embrace are real. They serve to inspire us to live life with purpose, to know that each and every one of us are important. May your faith be strengthened, refueled, inspired, encouraged, renewed, activated, or discovered. Each day is truly a precious gift from God. Welcome and come share with me a historical legend from *The Enchanting Legends of Shiloh Mansion*!

CHAPTER 1

It was a beautiful, warm, luscious, sunny, radiantly glowing, June morning. The garden looked delightfully enticing as all the gorgeous crepe myrtles were magnificently blooming in their showy flowering clusters of succulent, vibrantly tinted shades of pink and crimson! There were so many attractive, beautiful, stately trees amid the gardens at Shiloh Mansion. But it was just something ever so very special when the crepe myrtles bloomed so profusely. It had become an impending marvelous sign that summer was near.

Eliza had a breathtaking picturesque view from her sparkling, gleaming, beveled glass windows of one of her favorite spots in the garden. Here, in one of the many gardens of Shiloh Mansion, was the "gazebo of angels." The gazebo was elegantly accentuated in the same intricately scrolled wrought iron pattern that was on the gates leading to and surrounding Shiloh Mansion. The conspicuous gazebo stood ostentatiously tall, stately, open, and airy. Crowned within an open scroll wrought iron dome, it allowed the sun to shine brilliantly through by day or the elegant luminous moon to radiantly shine at night.

The gazebo also harmonized with the mansion's sturdy exterior walls that were made of limestone and marble. It was encircled by seven columns adorned with magnificently carved angels. Eliza would just come here sometimes to ponder, refuel, and sit just daydreaming or even bring her laptop and write profusely. Sometimes in the evening, she would simply gaze upward and admire the heavenly celestial skies! The gazebo was such a pleasant place. It had such a blissful serene openness about it that often led one to creative thought or simply to enjoy the pleasant environment amid the elegant gardens. This was also where Eliza, Faith, and Daniel often met before they would venture into the vast forest surrounding Shiloh Mansion.

Eliza lounged, slouching lazily, across her enormous comfy bed. Eliza loved her room; it was a great haven where she could get away from everything. Their mother had made sure that each of her children's bedrooms was decorated to their liking. It was not very often Eliza was able to just idly sprawl out and recline, but today was special. Her bed was lavishly adorned in soft satin brocade and plushy, velvet-quilted comfy comforter. It was in her many favorite colorful shades of pastel pinks and crimson, trimmed with braided metallic silver cording. It was festively decorated with lots of matching puffy down pillows that were plumped and stacked up next to her huge, massive, towering, antique mahogany headboard.

Shiloh Mansion was full of interesting, wonderful antiques spread generously throughout that had been carefully and personally selected by Eliza's mother, Lady Angelica. Eliza had two striking, matching antique French armoires in her bedroom. One of them had creatively been converted to keep her collectables and treasured keepsakes. Some of her many memorable keepsakes had come from their many expeditions whenever they had journeyed into the forest. Next to her window seat that overlooked the beautiful gardens was her attractive, intricately carved, antique desk. Here was where Eliza's sleekly designed, modern laptop—although seldom idle—rested on most evenings.

Although it was summer, she never allowed the staff to change her favorite comforter, unless of course if it was to be sent out to be dry-cleaned. It was just so comfy! Eliza had really come to simply love and appreciate it. She looked forward to the feeling she got whenever she plumped down on the cloud-soft, puffy, plush, down-filled comforter. It was her security blanket! Mother always had all their beds turned down in the evening time an hour or so before going to bed.

Eliza had a wonderful retreat in her bedroom en suite, delicately fitted with a chaise lounge and a pair of matching hot, pink, girly, upholstered boudoir chairs with an ottoman. It was a day to relax, even if only for a moment to pamper herself, doting happily atop of her bed. As Eliza lay there humming with her big, beautiful emerald-green eyes, she momentarily wedged her elbows between the pillows on the bed with her long, black wavy tresses hanging loosely and freely draping far beyond her long delicate gazellelike neck. Eliza, as all of the children, was pleasant to look upon. She had such a beautiful, warm, wonderfully deep-caramel-toned skin that was absolutely radiant! She was still quite unassuming as to just how pretty she really was.

Eliza had a wonder about herself. There was something that made her so interesting and appealing that you could not quite put your finger on. She was pleasant, often talkative, and could be very inquiring, yet not at all pushy. She often caught herself unconsciously gliding her long piano-friendly fingers over the smooth fabrics of her comforter. The soft billowy textures allowed her fingers to easily mimic gliding up and down the piano doing scales. She would joyously impersonate strumming out an étude or an arpeggio or sometimes a pop song or simply a tune of her own. Eliza had a beautiful voice and could sing just about anything, she loved music of all sorts and genres! Whenever she sang, her voice was mesmerizing!

Eliza and Faith, her younger sister, were almost inseparable; but sometimes, Eliza just liked spending time alone with herself. There was always so much going on in, around and about, Shiloh Mansion. So it was far and in between when she was able to get a few moments of carefree indulgence. Faith's room was actually right next door. As a matter of fact, they had adjoining suites. Between them, they shared a generously large, marvelous Jack-and-Jill bath wonderfully inland in marble.

They would both often open their doors to talk especially so in the summer when it was so nice and warm. Or one or the other would just cuddle and huddle up on each other's beds. It was nice that they were "sisters and friends." But since it was just the beginning of summer, she knew that Faith too was probably deep in thought herself, anticipating what would summer be like. She, of course, could not be sure. But Faith, she thought, was probably right now pondering upon what a marvelous time they would have today and is, perhaps sitting in her favorite comfy window seat, gazing out her big picture window, thinking about their soon upcoming, thrilling, anticipated adventure into the forest!

Sir Iverson, her father, and Lady Angelica knew that Faith was artistically imaginative. No doubt, Faith was a creatively gifted child. They were both such wonderful parents and quite intuitive! They were well aware of the unique temperaments of all their children. They did not expect her to be quite as scholarly as they anticipated Faith's two older siblings to be. Faith was pleasant, whimsical, capricious, joyful, amusing, and at times quiet. She was an adorable content child. She never really complained about much of anything. But oh, what a brilliant wonderful laugh; when she did, she would often laugh hysterically! She was quite mature beyond her years for a twelve-year-old.

Sir Iverson and Lady Angelica often wondered somewhat about Faith, there was something so very mystical about her. Eliza, Daniel, and Cousin Eva too knew that there was something very special about Faith. Eva simply adored Faith; because she was always so patient with her, nothing seemed to ruffle her feathers much. Eva would often come and just sit with her cuddling one of her many dolls. There was nothing at all uninteresting about Faith. She had a way of making people so comfortably at ease. Although sometimes serene, Faith was quite observant; and when necessary, she had no problem candidly telling anyone exactly how she felt.

Eliza always looked forward to summer too! For the first few days, it gave her chance to rest a bit from all the studying they had to do all throughout the semester. They had an arduous demanding schedule. Sir Iverson, her father, was adamant when it came to their studies. He expected Eliza, Faith, and Daniel to excel in their academics. Although busy, Sir Iverson and Lady Angelica were quite attentively involved in the lives of their children! The children were homeschooled by an exclusive professor who was fastidiously fussy when it came to their assignments.

Next to the downstairs library was their Wi-Fi learning room that opened to a large stone balustrade portico leading to the beautiful gardens. Here, they had all the latest imaginable interactive technology at their disposal! They had been educated as early as preschool in the latest advancements to enhance, nurture, and make their learning enjoyable and collaborative. On nice days when the weather was pleasant, they would take their studies outside in the afternoon. They had a lot of practical teachings incorporated into their studies that related to everyday living.

There was just something about the air around Shiloh Mansion. Sir Iverson and Lady Angelica had gone to great lengths to create an inside and outside environment that was welcoming and inviting. They lived an unbelievable harmonic lifestyle. They were quite aware of the benefits of having an estate-sized home; although enormous and stately, yet it still exudes such an elegant welcoming comfort and security!

Daniel was immensely brilliant! Although her elder brother Daniel surpassed Eliza in his natural excellence for studies, it did not bother her one bit. Sir Iverson expected them to do well and would not accept anything less, although he was a tad more flexible and lenient with Faith. There was no doubt that Sir Iverson was proud of all of his children. They had been well-groomed since birth. Smart technology was second nature to them! They were exposed to international lifestyles and governmental policies! This in itself broadened their scope of learning! But Daniel was an absolute exceptional genius as well as his only son. It only took a few moments of time conversing with him to discover that was in fact the case! What was so marvelous was that Daniel was not at all conceited or pretentious.

It was truly an absolutely gorgeous day as I mentioned earlier. Even though it was summer, Eliza still had much to do. Although there was no school in session, there was her ongoing music instructions. This took place year round. Practice she did! Most of the time, she really did not mind because she absolutely loved music. As a matter of fact, she loved all types of music. It was a wonderful delight to hear her play so gallantly and with such ease and perfection, she mastered the keys so brilliantly. She composed beautifully. But today, her focus was elsewhere. Today, she was looking forward again to a marvelous day of celebrating her new summer freedom! What child or teen does not like to take a break from school?

CHAPTER 2

Eva, their younger cousin, lived with them at Shiloh Mansion as well. Eliza, Faith, and Daniel all loved their little cousin Eva. But she was always getting into something. It was as though she was the bratty, little sister they never had. Her parents were not as strict when it came to Eva as well. Since Eva's parents were always traveling about somewhere, they seemed to make allowances for Eva. At times, she could be a bit annoying. But they realized that she missed her parents. When she was younger, she traveled with them; but now, she needed to have a suitable stable home life! Since she was an only child, she benefitted greatly from having the constant company of her cousins, who were more like her siblings.

Although Eva was seven years old, she still had a smidgen of baby chubbiness. She was cute as a button with her long frosty-colored hair, which was always adorned with a satin ribbon. She indeed was currently a permanent presence about Shiloh Mansion. She had caramel-colored skin with beautiful clear peridot-green colored eyes. As the sun began to set, her eyes seemed to take on a glow like a cat. Perhaps that was why she was always getting into something of mischief? Eva had such a very active and vivid imagination.

Eva had a splendid collection of dolls from all over the world. She usually had one in tow wherever she went. Her parents, Iris and Benjamin, would always send her dolls from wherever they traveled. It was almost like keeping a doll next to her was having a part of them with her. Eva's room was beautiful as well. Her bedroom was done in pastels, dominated by her favorite color, purple. Eva's bedroom walls were lined with shelves and were gracefully and tastefully festooned with her plethora of assorted dolls. She had a comfy brocaded window seat where she would sit and play with her dolls for hours at a time. Adjacent to her window seat was her table and chairs, where she had her many afternoon make-believe tea parties with, of course, her dolls and anyone else who would contentedly indulge her.

Eva also really loved animals. This really was not so unusual; after all, they had a private safari park adjacent to Shiloh Mansion. She could go and see the animals almost any time she wanted. But she just had to make sure that one of her older cousins was in attendance with her. The animals fascinated her so at the safari park. Altho was only opened from summer through fall for the pub for which many tourists traveled from all around the world to experience, the safari park was known as a state-of-the-art adventure!

One of Eva's frequent visitors was a huge, beautifully colored, blue-toned, exotic, rare bird, whom she had affectionately named Royal, who often sat tenaciously perched at her windowsill. She had chattered to him so that he often raucously mimicked her conversation.

Eliza was looking forward to an adventurous summer as usual. Just as she was beginning to prepare planning out her day while combing her long wavy ebony-black tresses she heard something. There was a knock at her door. It was Daniel. "Well," said Daniel. "What do you think about going to—"Before he could finish, Eliza's beautiful vivid emerald-green eyes lit up.

"Yes, yes of course, I was hoping that you would ask! Just give me a few moments, and I will meet you down at the gazebo. Will you go and tell Faith?"

"Sure!" said Daniel. "I have a few things to do, so let's meet in about an hour! Talk to you later."

As Daniel went to tell Faith, Eliza was so elated. She fell back on her bed and began to beam with exuberant happiness! Today, they were going to the forest and she was giddy with anticipation. The weather was exceptionally beautiful and no doubt they were in for a real treat.

lready opened when Daniel walked by,
her tenderly dangling one of her dolls
ith, I was going to ask if you would like
with us. But I see you have a visitor."

would love to go. I have been looking forward to us going for what seems like forever," said Faith.

"But I want to go," said Eva, listening in.

"Not this time," Daniel and Faith chimed in together.

"We are going to be there a while, and you will just get tired. When we come back, Eliza and I will have a tea party with you," said Faith.

"But I want to go," said Eva. Faith just looked at Daniel with raised eyebrows and sighed.

"I told Eliza that I had a couple of things to do, so we could meet in an hour or so?" said Daniel.

"That will work for me," said Faith.

Off down the long corridor to his masculine, cozy teen retreat went Daniel. He too had a relaxing comfortable bedroom, yet it was quite the contrast. Daniel's bedroom was his cocoon. It was done in rich, deep-dark-toned mahogany woods. There was mahogany wainscoting on the lower portion of the soaring walls of his room. His room was decorated in hues of his favorite color which was blue. Daniel's restful domicile den of a room was done in deep royal blue and a secondary color of forest green with a hint of sky blue throughout. His suite retreat had dark sienna-brown leather, nail-trimmed chesterfield demi sofa with two oversized matching masculine chairs. His desk dominated his retreat and over to the side was a table and four leather and suede chairs. Daniel's room, like all the other rooms within Shiloh Mansion, was of considerable size and tastefully appointed. Amid all the gracious antiques was the latest sophisticated interactive ultramodern technology!

As Daniel gallantly strolled down the corridor, it was evident that he was such a good-looking young man. It was quite interesting to see his striking transition. The older Daniel got, he walked straighter and taller just like Sir Iverson, his father, and looked more and more like him each day. Neither he nor his father was at all snobbish or pompous; but both of them were men of excellence and charm, no doubt confident and had every reason to be. Daniel had beautifully intense, piercing, rich light amber-brown eyes that glowed like a lion! He had a beautiful generous mane of ebony-black, curly, shoulder-length hair that was a little longer for boys his age. But it was always neatly trimmed. Daniel had this marvelous element of youthful style about him.

Eliza and Faith both respected Daniel. They looked up to their big brother. I think that had a lot to do with the way Lady Angelica had raised them. After all, he was the girls' only brother, and yes, older as well. He had also always heroically protected them on many occasions, especially so during their many escapades into the forest. Lady Angelica adored all her children and enjoyed them as well. But she also made sure that they were disciplined, courteous, and responsible. She realized that they should not take their many gifts and talents for granted. The Book of I Am says, "For unto whomsoever much is given, of him shall be much required" (Luke 12:48, KJV). When the children were babies, she personally attended to them patiently and tenderly. She was not overly stern or at all presumably passive.

Lady Angelica was a contented, talented, beautiful, strong woman. She had the most beautiful, deep dark, amethyst-colored eyes. She was witty, smart, funny, warm, loving, strong, compassionate, ladylike, and inviting. She has all the qualities any woman would ever want. Starting when the children were very young, she regularly read to them from the wonderful truths of the Book of I Am. She had such a marvelous joyous spirit about her.

It was a wonderful occurrence when the children were taught and learned many factual legends and principles of truth. It was important to Lady Angelica and Sir Iverson that they knew these foundational principles. Their lives were centered on the Great I Am! The children had been provided with a well-rounded, stable foundation. They did not take for granted the many blessings they enjoyed. They did quite well as a family, as well as having a prosperous flourishing family business. So much so that they had built on the grounds of Shiloh Mansion a beautiful temple as a tribute!

Did this mean that the children never got into trouble? No, they of course, every now and then, all had what I would call there "moments." But all in all, they had a wonderful camaraderie among themselves. There was an obvious noticeable cohesive and loving relationship between them. Shiloh Mansion had vast grounds and acreage surrounding them. I would not say that the children were isolated, because so many events and things were always going on or about them. There were many dinners in the grand formal dining room; and every now and then, there was a benefit ball or two—and there was the annual Christmas party. So there was someone always coming and going and/or visiting. The children also regularly participated in volunteering at a nonprofit in town as well as helped with planning the many benefits for their Alpha 7 Foundation!

Shiloh Mansion was about an hour drive from Canaan, which was the nearest city. The closest neighbors beyond the safari park were Mr. Leonard and his two children. They lived down in Forest Valley Mansion, which was also a grand estate. I think the children getting along so well had a lot to do with the many shared adventures they had around and about Shiloh Mansion. The way in which their parents related to them, as well as to one another, was also a huge contributing factor. Sir Iverson loved Lady Angelica, and there was no doubt that it was mutual! There was no uncertainty that Lady Angelica was the apple of his eye. Their family meant everything to them. They communicated openly and freely with their children and had an open-door policy, meaning they were always available. They were so accessible that any of the children could call, come in, or interrupt a business meeting if ever necessary.

When studies at Shiloh Mansion were in session, the children wore traditional uniforms. The uniforms consisted of classic burgundy, all-season wool, gabardine two-buttoned blazers with an embroidered family crest, oxford shirt, and ties. The girls wore TV ties, plaid skirts, or jumpers; and Daniel of course, slacks. Although home schooled, their studies often take them off-site to many other learning venue experiences. They also were assigned at times to observe and record statistics on the various animals at their neighboring safari park. After their studies for the day with Professor were completed, they could wear whatever they wanted. Daniel and all the other members in their family were always neatly and pleasantly groomed. This was true as well for the inside and outside staff at Shiloh Mansion.

There is a big production to the overall maintenance of Shiloh Mansion. Lady Angelica had selected a caring group of devoted people that managed the day-to-day operations making sure her home ran smoothly and efficiently.

Shiloh Mansion had immense acreage with rolling hills, beautiful manicured gardens and lawns along with many golden ponds inhabited by swans. Everything was always kept up so very nicely. Although it was a traditionally stylish, splendid palatial mansion, it was a pleasant place to live. Lady Angelica had always made it a point to tenderly care for her children. She made sure that they kept formal discipline as far as their studies.

Shiloh Mansion, although its facade is stately made in limestone and bountifully decorated with antiques, was still quite a comfortable living abode. Lady Angelica, as I said before, had impeccable taste; and her design signature was throughout their residential home. It was also equipped with all the latest and finest technological IT supercomputer advancements and integrated wireless devices. The mansion was fitted with every conceivable traditional and modern luxury available. Green technology, in fact, was Sir Iverson's forte. They loved and respected the environment both inside and outside. He was a first generation, well-respected IT mogul and had done an exceptional job!

"Oh my!" Daniel noted the time on his computer and realized that it was approaching the time for him to meet Eliza and Faith in the garden at the gazebo. From just looking at Daniel, you would never know; but Daniel had a remarkable gift. People, things, and objects were transparent to him. He could see straight through them in 3-D vision after a few moments of disciplined concentrated meditation. During one of their adventures while in the forest one day, he discovered he had another gift as well. Daniel is able to transform himself into an elevated altered state that renders him the ability to fly. When he initially discovered this, he would tumble awkwardly through the sky and fall to the ground. It was quite amusing. Now he had mastered his technique and could soar quite splendidly like a rocket.

"Hello, Daniel," it was Mother. Lady Angelica stood in the doorway to Daniel's room that was now ajar.

"What are you up to today, or should I say down to, on this beautiful summer day?" said Mother.

"Actually, I had talked to the girls earlier, and we are going for a walk. This being one of the few days we have before we start our summer schedule," said Daniel.

"Summer schedule?" said Mother. "You don't have a summer schedule."

"Well not really, but although our study sessions are completed, it gets pretty busy around here. So Eliza, Faith, and I have decided that we would take advantage of today and—"

"Okay, Daniel, I get your point. I have a letter from your Uncle Benjamin and Aunt Iris for Eva, and of course a package. So I am on my way to see little Eva," said Mother.

"That will be wonderful, because we are going to be out for a while and Eva wanted to tag along. So that will work out great for us. This way she will already be occupied and won't fret since we told her to stay at home," said Daniel.

"Just make sure that you all are back and ready in time for dinner this evening," said Mother.

"Yes, Mother," said Daniel. Daniel sort of smiled and tipped his head giving her a sort of cute, playful but respectful salute.

Daniel had now begun walking away down the long corridor again, on his way to meet Eliza and Faith at the gazebo. He was thinking about their adventurous excursion that lay ahead. Since Shiloh Mansion was the only home that the children had ever lived in, it was just a big comfortable home to them—not really a big deal. They were not impressed or in awe of it. It just happened to have every conceivable modern-day convenience one could imagine! They were also not inconsiderately cavalier about living in Shiloh Mansion when it came to others. Their parents had made it a point to provide them with a balanced environment, despite the fact that this was not the normal typical lifestyle for many. Only a select few had been able to attain this type of prominence and social standing.

Sir Iverson had worked very arduously and diligently in the field of technology and excelled above and beyond most. This was why he and Lady Angelica were adamant that they work hard at their studies and regularly participate in volunteering. She made sure that their life was balanced and well rounded as well. Nor did either of them want any of them to take life for granted! Time is precious; and no matter how much money one possessed, it cannot be bought. But they had discovered a way to maximize experiencing the past, present, and future!

Many people all over the world were facing some tough times in life! A mammoth amount of large corporations and businesses had gone under and financially collapsed! They continued to flourish and did much to contribute to the needs of others and the less fortunate! Family time was important to them! Sir Iverson, Lady Angelica, and all the children usually dined together for dinner as a family most evenings; dinner was at seven. Whenever Sir Iverson was away, he would Skype in and joined them wherever he was in the world!

As Daniel approached the mammoth, circular second-floor landing, he looked over and now in view was the grand, double-marble, gleaming grand-polished brass and wrought iron staircase. Shiloh Mansion was elegantly appointed like no other. Upon one's visiting, it was not at all too hard to be enamored somewhat. The marvelous, amazing views were breathtakingly beautiful from every room. Approaching the stately Shiloh Mansion, one encountered a long tree-lined road that led you through its gated manicured lawns. There was a beautiful, saltwater gunite pool that looked like an oasis along with a cabana. Several beautiful, sun-glistening golden ponds with swans were visible. And in the distance, there was a visible helipad surrounded by green pastures amid the background of the pictographic gardens and of course the gazebo of angels.

Leading up to the winding graceful driveway that crowned within the entry grand circle, there sitting upon a picturesque knoll was Shiloh Mansion. The mansion overlooked emerald-green pastures, studded with an assortment of beautiful towering trees. After ascending the seven balustrade stairs, one was faced upon entering Shiloh Mansion with beautiful, intricately designed, inlaid beveled glass and wrought iron, mahogany-trimmed double doors. The grand double-circular staircase was ornately exquisite. Overhead hung the massive Strass-Swarovski crystal chandelier, sparkling precision-cut diamond like crystals, in the three-story, glass-domed foyer rotunda. The natural dazzling light yielded an inviting, exposed stunning openness that one embraces upon entering the brilliant, imported marble foyer.

The three of them were all looking forward to their upcoming adventure. Daniel, Eliza, and Faith—although sisters and brother—they were really more like the modern-day three musketeers. They certainly were the high-tech twenty-first-century family. They were the generation "smart teens!" There was a smidgen of sibling rivalry from time to time; every now and then, they got into their congenial spats. But being raised by parents such as theirs at Shiloh Mansion was different. They did not spend a whole lot of time bickering. For the most part, besides being highly gifted and intelligent, they were quite normal children. They actually were a really great family. Lady Angelica and Sir Iverson were wonderfully great parents. They were indeed "the smart family!"

CHAPTER 3

Faith was patiently waiting and playfully meandering around in the gazebo. She looked fresh and summery! She had put on a pair of nicely creased linen, khaki-colored capri pants, and a multicolored jewel-tone top that set off her beautiful sapphire-blue eyes. As she leaned against one of the columns, she looked around and was just admiring the gardens and all the beautiful flowers that were in full bloom. Summer was such an exciting, splendidly beautiful time at Shiloh Mansion. But now, Faith was carried away deep in thought, thinking about the many legends Mother always read to them from time to time from the Book of I Am. They all knew that Mother rose early each morning for her "quiet time" and began her day by reading and meditating on the Book of I Am. One legend Faith had enjoyed in particular was the legend of this "young king." He had become a king at such a very early age. He was only eight years old when he actually took the throne. His name was Josiah!

Faith loved to read as well and thoroughly loved reading mysteries and fairy tales. She had a very creative imagination. She was such an intelligent, sensible child. There were many advantages living at Shiloh Mansion. But she could not ever begin to imagine herself having to give up her childhood to reign over a nation of people at such a young age. What an enormous responsibility! They had learned so many principles from the many historical legends. All of them enjoyed whenever Mother read to and with them from the Book of I Am. The legends were all so very fascinating, especially since they also knew they were all true! She had done this for as long as she could remember. This was even more so the reason they got excited. It was quite an intriguing adventure whenever they ventured into the luscious green forest and ascended one of the staircases that allowed them to actually enter the Enchanting Legends.

"You are already here," said Eliza anxiously as she was approaching the gazebo. "I took my time getting ready because today I was glad that I did not have to be on time for studies, do research, or complete my homework or—" Eliza had put on a pretty lace-lined shell with capped sleeves in her favorite color pink trimmed in the same color of her skirt. It matched beautifully with her khaki-colored skirt. Jangling nicely on her arm was a silver bracelet with tiny delicate rubies. As she turned standing, right behind her was Daniel; and he too had on khaki-colored slacks. He had on neatly pleated, creased pants and a blue shirt. They all kind of chuckled when they noticed they were coordinately matching. This happened all the time, which was also a sign they were on one accord. All the children were quite discerning! It was a tad uncanny how they knew what the other was thinking of. You never knew what was going to happen on their journey to the forest. Faith sort of knew, because she had such a keen, gifted insight of discernment. They were looking forward to their journey! She had already been thinking about the legend of the young king before Eliza and Daniel arrived.

One of the interesting things about living at Shiloh Mansion was that there was never a dull moment inside or outside. There was always something fun and adventurous to do. It was a huge, well-maintained place that contained a plethora of amenities. The staff was cordial, nicely accommodated, and quite comfortable as well; some were even provided charming living quarters nearby.

On the first floor of Shiloh Mansion was the library, the Wi-Fi learning center, breakfast room, solarium, enormous and inviting chef's gourmet kitchen, family formal dining room, atrium, estate-size formal dining room, billiard room, butler's pantry, fitness center, arcade and bowling alley. Adjacent to the game room, as well as a gentlemen's room, lady's spa retreat, parlor, grand ballroom, grand living room with towering cathedral ceilings, along with seven Italian marble fireplaces throughout the mansion, and of course, there was the grand double-marble-entry staircase, and the two-story domed foyer. Its second floor was open and airy. There was an elevator as well. Centrally located was the elegantly, intricately carved, beautiful woodwork landing railed in gleaming brass, mahogany, and wrought iron. This was also where the family's private living quarters were located. There was also a wing for the guest quarters with multiple, plentifully, tastefully appointed en suites and bathrooms.

Outside, one could almost taste the pristine freshness in the air at Shiloh Mansion. There was a stunning high-tech, self-cleaning gunite saltwater swimming pool, a spa with a massive stoned waterfall, a cabana, and a guesthouse. The magnificent gardens, manicured lawns, golden ponds, beautiful trees all add to the wonderful, healthy, naturally oxygenated environment. There were also tennis courts. Everything was always factitiously maintained. Every amenity one could possibly imagine was here! Shiloh Mansion was built far away from the usual pollution that was indicative of living in or near the city. They had an evolving, ongoing "going green environment." The staff had been educated in the benefits of recycling, preserving, and enhancing the quality of the overall environment. A fruitful recycling program was embraced and implemented throughout Shiloh Mansion.

The environment about Shiloh Mansion was warm and inviting. As I said earlier, all of the children's bedrooms were custom decorated to their liking. Each of their rooms was reflective of their personal, unique temperaments and desired color palette. This was important to Lady Angelica since Shiloh Mansion was so large. She wanted her children to feel free, at home, and comfortable amid the quiet luxury. In spite of it being such an enormous domicile, it was still simply their home. When not imbibing in any of the many possible activities available, they all gladly retreated to their ample suites.

Today, Cook had packed each of them a generous picnic lunch to carry with them. This way they did not have to come back for a set lunchtime. With their special custom backpacks in tow, they could just leisurely take their time. At some point, they would take out time to eat. They were so excited! Shiloh Mansion was surrounded with oodles of beautiful, charming pictorial spots to do just that. Mother had already reminded them to just make sure that they were back in time for dinner. Now, since the children were older, they also had a lot more freedom when studies were not in session. Shiloh Mansion was a secure sanctuary to wonder about and having a wireless security system made it just that much safer. Of course, they each as usual always carried their smartphones.

It was once they entered the surrounding outer forest where they had to be carefully vigilant. They were thoroughly aware of the many possible dangers which lurked in the forest. They were also mindful that the world was continuously becoming more wicked since so many were turning away from the principles in the Book of I Am. There were many catastrophic natural disasters happening all throughout the world. The economic status of many countries was continuously dwindling! Many, many families had been impacted financially! However, their family remained privileged, quite abundantly, financially sound. This was something that they had been taught not to ever take for granted! They were quite fortunate and blessed to have parents of integrity that were respected.

Having a safari park at Shiloh Mansion kept the children abreast of the animals that lived in the wilds. There was an immense expanse of hundreds of natural acreage. There was a vast assortment of animals from Africa and all around the world. The animal habitat represented omnivores, herbivores, and carnivores and a huge selection of reptiles and exotic birds within the park.

The animals were securely fenced within beyond a wireless state-of-the-art smart alarm system. A humongous expansive aviary for the exotic birds was provided. They had gone to great lengths and made grand strides to create a natural habitat at the safari park. There was little or minimal human contact with some of the animals in order to preserve their natural instincts and behaviors. These animals had not been tamed. They were allowed to roam freely in their own domicile. But of course, over time, they had become a tad more docile to a degree, since they were exposed to seasonal touring visitors.

There was also a huge interactive community section where the more docile animals were kept! Here, they also research and teach wildlife propagation and the importance of preserving wildlife. They teach respect for the preservation of the animals, their ecosystems, and their origins of which, all of us inhabiting this planet, share. In the Book of I Am, they learned that the first man Adam actually named all the animals in the very beginning of time. So they respected their territory. Tours were open and available to the public from June to October. It was not at all unusual to see busloads of children along with their teachers. During this season, there was additional physical security to maintain the safety of the visitors as well as make sure that the family's residential privacy remained intact.

On the way to the forest, they passed by the chapel. It was such a pleasant, tranquil, nice sanctuary. Sir Iverson had it built on the grounds of Shiloh Mansion. They were not ritualistic or legalistic but quite adamant in honoring the Lord. It was a charming, quaint but noble chapel built with the same elegance of Shiloh Mansion as a gift to Lady Angelica from Sir Iverson. She was devoted to the Lord and frequented the sanctuary regularly as did all the family. It was really no different than someone having dedicated a private prayer room in their own home. The land surrounding Shiloh Mansion was quite vast so for them having a chapel was quite appropriate. Here, one could sense a closeness with nature and a still inviting presence with one's Creator. The chapel was always open and a tranquil, peaceful, relaxing place to go meditate and commune, surrounded by a gorgeous rose garden. It too was maintained by the staff at Shiloh Mansion and open to them as well. Often the local place of worship in the city was quite full of activity and often crowded. It was also an hour's drive away.

Lady Angelica and Sir Iverson were dedicated to their faith, and they trusted the Lord. So much so that they named there last born daughter Faith. During her pregnancy with Faith, Lady Angelica had to remain on bed rest most of her last trimester. Shiloh Mansion for her was a most quiet, serene retreat during this time. The benefits and functions that Lady Angelica had planned to take place at Shiloh Mansion were rescheduled. At this time, she was also closely monitored. Rather than stay in the hospital, she was able to do so with an attending live-in private nurse at Shiloh Mansion. The nurse had at her disposal all the medical paraphernalia necessary to professionally attend to Lady Angelica. This also allowed her to stay close to her family as well. Lady Angelica was first advised by her doctor not to go full term, because it was considered a high-risk pregnancy. She had experienced placental abruption. This would cause great discomfort at times to Lady Angelica.

Placenta abruption is when the placenta begins to partially peel away from the uterine wall. It can also possibly deprive the baby of necessary nutrients and oxygen and is known to cause bleeding in the mother as well. Placenta abruption can often present a threat to both mother and child.

Eliza was but a little toddler when Faith was born. Since Lady Angelica was on bed rest while carrying Faith, both Eliza and Daniel were able to spend a lot of quality time just being with their mother. Although she rested, she also spent a lot of time with her children. Daniel often ventured around and about the Shiloh Mansion estate. Eliza stayed close by her mother with an attending nanny nearby when needed. She remembered how she got a chance to hear many times the sound of her sister's heartbeat while in her mother's tummy. She could see and feel her moving about as well as see how she grew on the monitor. She asked her mother, "When is she coming out? When do I get to see my sister?"

"Soon," her mother would say. Eliza would often carefully cuddle up with Mother in the afternoon for her nap as she waited. So, it was of no surprise that she and Faith were very close after she was born. She had excitedly anticipated her baby sister's arrival. She vicariously shared the experience with her mother. It was quite common because children were able to empathize and feel what we feel. Their natural insight and heightened emphatic abilities were extraordinary when they had been raised in a loving, warm, free environment. During the pregnancy, Eliza and her mother would talk to Faith; and together, they would hum and sing such lovely duets, lullabies, and nursery songs to her.

Faith was born an adorable, beautiful, healthy, petite baby girl with a head full of hair. Her rare, brilliant sapphire-blue eyes, caramel skin, and now long striking black hair and serene temperament made for an interesting package. Faith too had an unusual gift. All of Lady Angelica's children had a beautiful, assorted palette of gemstone eye colors. Beyond Faith's eyes was a mind of creative imagination. Faith was later to learn she had a special gift and could imagine super talented characters that would come to life whenever she senses danger. The characters were not seen by anyone else except Eliza and Daniel. That was unless she desired for them to be visible to others. To some, they might be considered angels. Finally, Lady Angelica and Sir Iverson had been through a lot and was thankful that they had been so generously provided for. Their business and investments had yielded generous, assured, financial, lifelong stability for future generations as well. They in turn gave generously to and supported many charities.

As the children were blissfully walking, you could hear their footsteps in the quietness, with eager anticipation as they were nearing the beautiful, lush outer grounds of Shiloh Mansion. It was here, at this point, that they passed by the chapel that was surrounded in a breathtaking picturesque landscape. In passing, they all waved merrily to Minister David. Minister David was the minister and spiritual advisor to Sir Iverson and Lady Angelica. He was a boldly spoken forward yet cordial man who always seemed to have a smile on his face. He lived in the abbey near the chapel that was adjacent to Shiloh Mansion. On the weekend, he was usually in the city of Canaan overseeing the clergy conducting worship services. He did this as well on several occasions during the week.

Back at Shiloh Mansion, Lady Angelica was sitting and talking to little Eva. Eva still had not realized that the older children had already departed. She of course was excited and full of chatter, because there was a much-welcomed note from her parents. They would often have a live Skype visit on the computer; but whenever there was a package, there was a letter! It always contained the usual questions about how was she doing and how her studies were and how proud they were of her and how much they missed her. Eva took her time slowly opening the package. First, she gently tore away the brown shipping packaging and removed the tissue paper that revealed a beautifully wrapped box. This time it was even in her favorite color purple with a silver bow. She blushed and smiled as she carefully and hurriedly removed the pretty paper. There lying among more layers of tissue was another brand new doll.

Eva was almost losing count of just how many dolls she had since there were so many! There was her favorite doll "Baby" that she always carried with her. "Oh, she is so beautiful!" said Eva. Her beautiful eyes lit up! Aunt Angelica had brushed her beautiful frosted hair earlier, and she had ever so neatly tied in a purple ribbon. Purple was her favorite color. Eva's hair was lighter by contrast to all of them since Lady Angelica, Sir Iverson, and all their children had dark, curly, and wavy tresses. Although equally beautiful, their hair again was a rich dark almost ebony black. Eva, on the other hand, had light-colored peridot-green eyes just like her mother Iris. She too had dimpled cheeks, but Iris was fair-skinned, and was a tad chubby.

"Oh, she is so beautiful," cried Eva again. As she picked her up, "She looks like Eliza, Faith, and you, Aunt Angelica! Except she has my eyes! I think I will call her...I don't know! I have so many now!" she chimed innocently in a high-pitched, excited voice.

"I...well, you will have plenty of time to think of a name for her," said Aunt Angelica as she smiled. "Now that it is summer, I am sure the two of you will have plenty of time to get acquainted with one another. So why don't you go and introduce her to the rest of your lovely family? I think that we will just have to plan a playtime with a couple of your friends?" said Lady Angelica. Eva lit up again, she liked that idea!

"I will go right now, I want Eliza and Faith to see her," said Eva.

Aunt Angelica quickly responded and said, "I mean all your other little—"

"Oh, you mean Baby and my other dolls?"

"Yes!" said Aunt Angelica. Aunt Angelica realized that the children had already left for their excursion and were too far along for Eva to catch up with them. Anyway, they had already told her that she could not come along.

The older children were all quite fond of Eva. She was actually at times the bratty little sister they did not have. But today, they really did not want her to tag along. They were going far beyond the safari park! "I think I will sit with her at my window seat and let her get to know Baby first," said Eva.

"I think that is a great idea, I will have Cook send up your lunch. Would you like that? This way you can take your time getting to know your new little—"

"Oh, thanks, Aunt Angelica, that will be great!" replied Eva. On that note, Aunt Angelica gracefully left as Eva began toward the window seat. The window seat was one of her favorite spots in her whole room.

* * *

"We are almost there," said Eliza. "Perhaps we should eat our lunch before we actually get to the forest?"

"I think that is a good idea," said Daniel. "I am getting a tad hungry from all the walking!" Faith eagerly nodded her head in agreement.

At this point, they could no longer see Shiloh Mansion. But they could now see, across the way, the densely wooded Forest Valley Mansion Estate. This was an indication that they were quite close to the entrance of the forest. It is here at Forest Valley Mansion where Mr. Leonard lived along with his two children. He was the father of James and Rhonda. Mr. Leonard was very stern and often somewhat controlling. He was quite the pretentious person, not really a bad man. But he could be a bit snobbish and often shrewd in his business affairs. At one time, he had been a lot friendlier and outgoing. Their father had told them he had become a somewhat embittered man shortly after his wife died unexpectedly of cancer. He gradually began to distance himself from everyone and was now a bit more reclusive.

The Forest Valley Estate was much more remotely located. There was plenty of land surrounding the estate home at Forest Valley Mansion. It was quietly nestled in the midst of lots of tall, intense, dense beautiful trees. It was much different from Shiloh Mansion. It was a Tudor-style mansion with extensive sprawling acreage. There were formal gardens, a tennis court, pond, swimming pool, and greenhouse; and there was even a tall gated maze. But it was walled in and a much older-style estate. There was an ominous, gloomy-like presence, sort of like it was almost in mourning. It just did not have the open, airy, fresh, invigorating feel that one experienced when approaching Shiloh Mansion. It was also filled with beautiful antiques of course. It just did not have that welcoming feeling one got when being at Shiloh Mansion nor was it equipped with all the latest technology as well! Mr. Leonard's family had been in the fine furniture business for generations and had continued to do quite well.

Forest Valley Mansion, however, was darker, a bit rustic, and hidden away by its dense foliage. It really seemed more like an old museum than a home. It had a cottage that was just about covered with ivy for the staff, and it also even had a log cabin for the maintenance crew, which gave it a somewhat dated ambience. It was not as warm, elegant yes, but colder with dark-wood-paneled walls not at all inviting like Shiloh Mansion. It was just different! Nor did Forest Valley have a host with the grace their mother exuded. Lady Angelica contributed well to making their home so appealing and engaging. You could feel the genuine love between Lady Angelica and Sir Iverson. He still kissed her whenever they parted company and whenever he returned, and it wasn't just for show. It was of no surprise to see them momentarily embrace in passing. Lady Angelica often lovingly hugged her children as well. The Book of I Am often talked about the importance of marriage and family.

There was such a polarized contrast between the two gentlemen and their families. Mr. Leonard had raised his children alone after his wife had died. His family's wealth had come from the booming furniture empire his great, great grandfather had built. Mr. Leonard was a tall, lean man of medium build and had chestnut-brown/gray hair and chestnut-brown eyes. He always looked quite serious and preoccupied often deep in thought. He did not seem to be approachable at all. Mr. Leonard relied a lot on Ms. Hillary. She came on board shortly before Mrs. Leonard had passed years ago. Ms. Hillary oversaw the household at "Forest Valley Mansion." She secretly loved Mr. Leonard; but realized that because of their different places in society, they will probably never marry. She continually tried to help James and Rhonda often to no avail. They both were intelligent children but were always getting into much mischief. Most of it was for attention-getting purposes, but it seemed to go right over their father's head. Mr. Leonard was dreadfully blind to their many deceptions.

Rhonda, Mr. Leonard's only daughter, was fiery and had flaming red, carrot-topped hair. She usually tried to dominate her older brother, James. She was terribly indulged and really quite narcissistic; to put it bluntly, she was just plain spoiled and self-centered! She was totally oblivious as to how others feel. Rhonda was fourteen years old. That was really the only thing she had in common with Eliza. They were totally opposite. Mr. Leonard's son, James, was smart, crafty, contentious, often annoying and a bit cunning; and he too was sixteen like Daniel. He too had chestnut-brown hair like his father except that he had coal-black eyes. They both were very competitive with Daniel and Eliza. Rhonda and James had accompanied their father to Shiloh Mansion on many occasions. Eliza felt compassion for Rhonda since she essentially had no mother and always hoped that she would change. She could not imagine not having a mother such as hers.

"Well, this looks like a really great spot for lunch," said Daniel. So they all plopped down in the grass and fell back momentarily looking up in the luminous summer sky. Cook had prepared a delicious picnic lunch of white albacore tuna salad on whole multigrain wheat bread with shredded romaine, sides of celery sticks, baby carrots, avocado, fresh fruit cocktail, chips, peanut butter cookies, and fresh lemonade along with bottled water for each of them, all neatly packed in their monogrammed eco-friendly backpacks. Their backpacks were trimmed in aeronautic-grade, high-quality reflective silver so they could be easily found! Each of them had a smartphone and DVD, 3-D Blue-ray player with Wi-Fi, which their custom backpacks had an attached holder for.

"Let's say grace. And let's dig in, I'm hungry," said Eliza. Then she turned on some music. Remember, Eliza loved music!

"Let's thank God for our food," said Faith. "Father, you alone are God and above you is no other. You have made the skies, the heavens, the earth, and the seas; and everything in them, for this we thank you. Protect us and keep us as we enter into the land of the Enchanting Legends. And now for the strength and nourishment of our bodies, we thank you for this food we are about to receive, in the name of Jesus, amen!"

"Amen!" said Eliza and Daniel.

As they gingerly ate lunch, they discussed and merrily chatted of all the fun things that they wanted to do this summer. This was Daniel's last summer before he would be going off to the university. It had not yet been decided where he would attend. But one thing he did know was that he was going to make a point to enjoy every bit of his last leisurely summer.

CHAPTER 4

"I'm full!" said Faith. It didn't take too much to fill Faith because she was such a modest yet health conscious eater. She also ate rather slowly, took tiny bites, and took countless chews before actually swallowing her food. This was also why she had always remained slender!

Faith was usually quite practical; but today, she was giddy and excited! It had been a while since she had been to the Enchanting Legends, and now they were just a few minutes away. Since she was so creative, it was also always a treat to actually be venturing into the forest. There was something so mysterious and yet electrifying about the many sounds and all the various shrubbery and massive trees as they brushed against her arms as they walked. It tickled her heart and gave her a warm secure feeling. As she strolled along the nature trail, Faith could vividly imagine the characters that Mother so often had read to them about from the Book of I Am. Faith had such a creative imagination, so she was looking forward to stepping into the days of yore. Here they learned so much. History interestingly so became alive and their appreciation for life grew that much more. It was always such an incredible journey. They knew that time was precious.

"I'm done too," said Eliza. Daniel just kept on eating and munching, nodding his head. Daniel often had a ferocious appetite. He ate properly, but he really could put away some food. He was a great swimmer, and it was evident by his physique that he had mastered the technique of burning calories. No doubt it had a lot to do with his brain that always seemed to be thinking of something imaginative and innovative to do as well! He seemed as though he was getting taller as they watched. This year he had an enormous growth spurt and was now more than a full head and shoulders taller than the girls.

The girls could tell Daniel was not ready to close his backpack. So the girls just looked at one another, laughed, pointed, and said together, "He's not."

The children collectively had an incredible assortment of gifts! One in particular was that all three of them were time travelers! Whenever they entered into the forest, there were three mystical staircases that led them into the land of the Enchanting Legends. It was here that the stories from the Book of I Am and the characters virtually came alive! They could transcend time and enter into a portal leading to the past, present, and/or future! There was a hidden secret portal also at Shiloh Mansion, but it was rarely ever used. It really was to be used in the event there was an extreme emergency. Entering from the forest better prepared them for transitioning into their time journey excursion.

This was why the children were so excited! They stepped into another dimension and were actually able to travel back and forth in time! They could step into a vortex that opened at the top of the staircase and allowed them to experience the many past legends firsthand. The legends from the Book of I Am were true episodes of events that actually took place in history.

They had been studying about "the young king" and were looking forward to perhaps meeting him on one of their journeys. This historical legend had so fascinated them, because it let them know that someone much younger than themselves and slightly a little older than Eva had actually become a king and reigned over a nation. What an interesting responsibility that this must have been! The young king was Josiah. This was why Faith was in such deep thought back at the gazebo of angels. They also knew and realized that fewer and fewer people believed or continued to read the potent, compelling Book of I Am. It was not the popular thing to do as much now for some. But they knew for sure that within its contents were the keys that unlocked wisdom and the mysteries of the true meaning of life! It was the "Book of the Living Truth!"

Each time they had entered into the land of the Enchanting Legends, they returned home much wiser and more appreciative. They were truly able to grasp the essential importance of life. They knew the precious, significant, priceless value of time! This in fact was why they were so motivated and much more encouraged to make a joint concerted effort to reach their full potential while living on earth. They had been given gifts. But with those gifts came huge responsibilities. They toiled hard and long at their studies. Yet, they still played hard and gleefully, enjoying themselves as children. Sir Iverson and Lady Angelica made it a priority to create and nurture an environment where the children could grow mentally, spiritually, emotionally and academically. It was important to them as parents that they know how to favorably interact with people and the world around them. It was a priority that they actually implement the many principles that they had learned within their personal lives from the Book of I Am.

Sir Iverson and Lady Angelica, as their parents, realized that there was a tremendous spiritual battle going on; and that we all virtually lived in a spiritual multidimensional war zone. They knew that it was important to always be adorned with the "spiritual armor." Fear was not a part of the armor. This was also why they were able to meander about so freely. Their children were now of age. Their parents expected them to be responsible and told them that they were on "God watch," meaning that wherever they were they knew and were mindful that God was omnipresent! And especially whenever they ventured into the forest, they must be extremely discerning and careful. Once in the forest, they were beyond the security system of Shiloh Mansion. Their parents realized and were confident that wherever they were, regardless as to what was going on, God was with them. But still, they needed to be mindful of their surroundings and be responsible and careful! They also realized that God was always ultimately in control of everything.

This was also why they were so conscientious even though they were still children. They all were mature beyond their years! It was this same maturity that made it possible for Josiah to reign as king at eight years old. Yet of course, their parents also knew that because of this there was a great opportunity for them to be tempted and pulled from their center and become unfocused. That much danger lurked as well because of the war between the powers that be and the principalities. The prince of the power of the air had imps all over the place. So they really strived to create a balance for the children. They had taken the necessary human precautions and also trusted the Lord. They would not be hindered and refused to live being fearful. But yes of course, wise and at times cautious. They were aware that they were under watchful eyes waiting to catch them off guard and acting out of their character! They were also aware that the imps had many sophisticated ways of trying to entice, deceive, and entrap them.

As I said earlier, Shiloh Mansion had the latest security technology which was closely monitored. They were allowed to enter the forest and were tracked by GPS on their smartphones. They also had invisible GPS wristbands that became activated when they were time traveling! GPS is a satellite-tracking system that works in any weather twenty-four hours a day. The results were forecasted on an electronic map! The security around the mansion was quite sophisticated as well, and they were alerted when or if a stranger had entered or wandered onto the grounds of Shiloh Mansion.

Now since they all had reached the age of accountability, they had the right to wander freely! They were usually pretty responsible and also knew that there would be consequences for their actions. Yes, they were still children; but they had been well schooled and knew to the degree they put into practice what they learned, there was no need for alarm. They knew that they were under God watch! This was what made it so beautiful. They had been taught that with privileges came responsibilities. Again, "To whom much is given, much is required!" (Luke 12:48, KJV).

In the Book of I Am, they had learned how the Lord had made a promise to Abram (Abraham) in regards to the land, and that he would be blessed and so would the subsequent generations after him. This would be possible if he would follow the Lord! This was the promise he made to Abram, "Leave your country, your people, and your father's household and go to the land I will show you" (Genesis 12:1, NIV).

GOD'S PROMISE TO ABRAHAM

I will make you into a great nation and I will Bless you;
I will make your name great, and you will be a blessing.
I will bless those who bless you, and whoever curses you
I will curse; and ALL peoples on the earth will be Blessed through you!

Genesis 12:2-4 (NIV)

Abram was seventy-five years old when he left to go to the land that the Lord had shown him which was called Canaan! There were already people in the land that were not friendly called the Canaanites, but the Lord told him not to be afraid. He assured him that he would be with him. That the land would surely be given to his offspring! It was not until his later years that Abraham and his wife Sarah actually became parents. This in itself was a miracle, because it was way after his wife, Sarah, was far beyond the age of childbearing that she became pregnant. Abram was a man of great faith who trusted in the Lord!

The Lord later changed his name to Abraham. He confirmed his covenant to bless him saying, "And when Abram was ninety years old and nine, the Lord appeared to Abram and said unto him, I am the Almighty God; walk before me, and be thou perfect. And I will make a covenant between me and thee, and will multiply thee exceedingly" (Genesis 17:1-2, KJV). "And Abram fell on his face and God talked with him saying, As for me, behold my covenant is with thee, and thou shalt be a father of many nations. Neither shall thy name any more be Abram but thy name shall be called Abraham; for a father of many nations have I made thee. And I will make thee exceedingly fruitful, and I will make nations of thee and kings shall come out of thee: and I shall establish my covenant between me and thee and thy seed after thee in their generations for an everlasting covenant, to be a God to thee and to thy seed" (Genesis17:3-7, KJV).

The Land Promised, Renewed

"The land wherein thou art a stranger, all of the land of Canaan, for an everlasting possession; and I will be their God. And God said unto Abraham, Thou shalt keep my covenant therefore, thou, and thy seed after thee in their generations. This is my covenant, which ye shall keep, between me and you and thy seed after thee" (Genesis 17:8-10, KJV). In turn his descendants and future generations were to keep this covenant with the Lord! The Lord, later on, actually sent angels to visit with Abraham and his wife, Sarah, to tell them when they would have a baby. As mentioned earlier, this would be a memorable miracle, because Sarah was beyond the usual age of childbearing. She actually laughed at the thought of bearing a child at such an old age, she was at the age of ninety when she finally gave birth! Sarah's name was actually changed by God's request from Sarai to Sarah (Genesis 17:15, KJV)! They were also told to name the happily expected child Isaac. This established the covenant the Lord had with Abraham!

Sir Iverson and Lady Angelica had read the history of Abraham to their children on many occasions! They fully believed and embraced the principles of this covenant and taught them to their children. This was why they were so very successful! The narrative of Abraham and his family was another great legend from the Book of I Am.

This was the very reason why there was something so very indescribably special when approaching Shiloh Mansion that one could not quite put their finger on. It was an all-around, spiritually harmonic environment! This land represented to them the fulfillment of the promise that the Lord made to Abraham. They honored the Lord and welcomed his presence in their home and surrounding expansive grounds. They were of course now, thousands of years later, part of the future generations that realized that the earth was the Lord's! They respectfully embraced the Lord's principles for life and living! This was why their family had such a respect for nature, love of people, and concern for the environment as well as respect for the Book of I Am. There was true love, care, trust, and concern between them as a family. Time was precious and priceless! This was also the true reason for Sir Iverson's success in the technology field and the beautiful, peaceful abode Lady Angelica had created for them at Shiloh Mansion. His priorities were right. The Book of I Am also taught them that it was God who gave the power to get rich. And rich they were. Not just materially but in every way. They all believed and knew firsthand how very important and significant all the legends really were!

Once in the land of the Enchanting Legends, their spiritual gifts were also remarkably enhanced. It was here the people actually value the Book of I Am! They realized that God was the all-powerful God of Abraham, Isaac, and Jacob! That he was truly the only God Most High!

Daniel, the eldest child, had been taught the principles of the Book of I Am from birth. He, in his own right, was already a genius. His gifts and talents had been nurtured by his parents. He now had the power to see through people, objects, or buildings, and could change his form. The ability to change forms gave him the ability to also soar. Daniel had a marvelous singing voice as well!

Eliza had a tremendous gift of discernment and readily recognized the presence of evil. She was not one to be easily deceived! Eliza also was multitalented, and she had a tremendous, melodious, beautiful singing voice and played many musical instruments. She could make music out of just about anything. She was aware of another legend about King Saul. He was a king who turned away from the Lord's teachings. The spirit of God left him, and he needed David to play his harp to calm his fears and anxiety! This legend is found in 1 Samuel 16: 14-23. David eventually became one of the greatest kings of Israel. Eliza knew the power within music!

Faith was multitalented also and able to sing and communicate with nature, animals, and the wind through her multimusical abilities. She could calm a baby or incite or quiet a ferocious lion. This was also why her cousin Eva loved her company. Together, they were a dynamic trio with endless capabilities! Faith was quite creative as well, she was able to close her eyes and imagine the ministering angels that came in view whenever she sensed danger. She was actually praying unceasingly. The angels were not seen by anyone else except Eliza and Daniel, unless they desired for them to be visible to others. They could allow them to see through their eyes. Faith was very serene and humble. I think it had a lot to do with all Lady Angelica went through while she was carrying her in the womb.

Daniel, Eliza, and Faith all also had the fruit of the Spirit that is love, joy, peace, long-suffering, gentleness, goodness, faith, meekness, and self-control operating within their character. The Book of I Am talks about the fruit of the Spirit as well in a marvelous book called Galatians (Galatians 5:22).

Altogether, Daniel, Eliza, and Faith made an interesting trio. This was why they were the "smart teens!" Now it was easy to understand how they were also known as the three musketeers. They knew that there was power in unity. Working together cohesively, they could really accomplish much! Faith and her love of mysteries and fairytales had come to enjoy the well-known story of the French historical novel by Alexandre Dumas. *Les Trois Mousquetaires*, interpreted *The Three Musketeers*, was one of them! They all were well rounded in their studies and had studied many of the historical classics. Not so much for the story line itself but because of the relationships and interconnected friendship the trio shared. They all had marvelous, loyal relationships as siblings. They took seriously and honored the covenant pact between themselves. They lived by the motto "All for one and one for all." Although time travelers, they were still children and family who enjoyed most of the things that other children enjoy. This was why they had an arcade, bowling alley, theater, and yes, now you understand, the gazebo of angels at Shiloh Mansion.

Their mother, Lady Angelica, had faithfully instilled in them a firm belief in the Book of I Am. Because of this, their faith, trust, and belief in the Lord—the God Most High— was so strong. They were not legalistic or unyielding but kind, loving, good hearted, disciplined, and open minded.

They had a pretty good understanding in regards to the purpose of life. They had fervently studied the historical correct Book of I Am along with their many other subjects on their laptops. The Acts of the Apostles this last semester was studied in religion class with Professor. It was here they discovered many of the actual acts of kindness and healings that were wrought through the disciples of Jesus. This was not an elective study. It was a part of their core general curriculum requirements of history, language, math, and animal ancestry studies. Although Lady Angelica personally had an authentic, rare, original copy of the Book of I Am, they also had access via modern technology on their laptops as well as a plethora of authentic translations. Here they had learned the many marvelous things that took place as well as the miracles the apostles had accomplished. It was from here they gained much wisdom and spiritual insight.

As the three of them entered the densely populated forest and reached the designated spot, Eliza took out her pouch of silver sparkles and then sprinkled them about. A translucent mystical staircase crystallized and appeared as they raised their hands and said, "*You shall receive power when the Holy Spirit has come upon you.*" The Greek word for "power" is *dunamis*, which is potential power or ability. *At this time, their faith was reenergized and activated! They were now able to see into the spiritual dimension all about them! This phrase came from the book of Acts1:8 (*NIV*) in the Book of I Am.*

The time had come for them to begin to ascend the spiral staircase. Eliza again took the silver sparkles and sparingly sprinkled each of them about. As they ascended a swirling vortex, the sky began to open; and now they, along with their clothing, were now beginning to become transformed in order to appropriately enter the land of the Enchanting Legends of Shiloh Mansion!

CHAPTER 5

"Every time we travel to another era in time, it's very wonderfully different. It is so very amazing!" said Faith. Faith looked around in wonder and marveled. "Each time it is just so splendidly fascinating! Are we there yet? Have we reached our destination?" said Faith. The children had now entered an actual era of the Enchanting Legends. As I said earlier, they have been gifted with the amazing ability to time travel. They were now in and about the city of Jerusalem. Josiah reigned thirty-one years as king of the nation of Judah. His name means healed by Jehovah God. During his lifetime, he actually instituted major reforms as a ruler and king. He ordered Priest Hilkiah to revitalize and restore the temple, which was dedicated to God, by using money raised from taxes. It was here during this time travel journey that they would see firsthand what it was like for him to rule. Although not exactly certain at what age they would see him, they knew that they would experience the era of the young king.

Josiah was known for being a great ruler of Judah. He took the throne at the early age of only eight years old. The children had thoroughly studied the Book of I Am, so they somewhat knew what to expect. But actually, being there was still utterly amazing. Each time they entered an era was still quite intriguing and unexplainable! They never knew exactly where or what the precise date was, but they somewhat had an idea; time travel is not an exact science! But since they had studied thoroughly, they knew to some extent what to expect!

Josiah's life as the young king was recorded in the Book of I Am in 2 Kings 22 and 2 Chronicles 34. The boy king believed in the Lord and consulted him for direction. He was called to rule during a difficult and tumultuous period of time. During the time of his rule, the international relationships about them were in great despair. Josiah, however, honored God and was actually the last good king to rule over the southern kingdom. "He did what was right in the eyes of the Lord and walked in the ways of his father, David, not turning from the left or to the right" (2 Chronicles 34, NIV). There were four kings to reign after him. However, they were all very wicked, brutally mean, and did not honor the Lord. Eliza, Faith, and Daniel had learned in history that King Josiah was to eventually meet an untimely death.

The Book of I Am, taught us that after King Solomon's death there was a great revolt! Israel was united when they were under the rule of King David and also later under his son King Solomon. They were a great nation of tribes, but the brothers and their relatives constantly warred among themselves. There was a continuing, underlying tension going on between them. That tension was never resolved and eventually escalated, which resulted with the tribes splitting! Then the northern and southern regions formed two separate nations. What is so interesting is the nation of Israel actually consisted of the twelve tribes that originally came from the twelve sons of Jacob! Jacob was later named Israel!

King Solomon left a mighty prosperous empire! Rehoboam, the son of King Solomon, became king of the southern kingdom after his father died. He had two tribes, which was called Judah! Jeroboam, the son of Nebat, became king over the northern kingdom. He had the ten remaining tribes, which was called Israel. Instead of following the Lord and the Book of I Am, both kings did what was good in their own eyes rather than listened to God.

Many prophets were sent by the Lord to advise the kings of both Israel and Judah. God warned them through his prophets and seers. However, they continually slid more and more into idolatry—worshipping false gods, immorality, disobedience, and rebelliousness! They did not listen nor consult the Book of I Am. The divisions between the kingdoms lasted for many centuries. The consequences were great! After this, the children of Israel eventually were taken into Babylonian captivity.

Josiah's grandfather, Manasseh, was a young king as well! But he was wicked and did not honor God. There were many horrible, disturbing stories about his grandfather Manasseh! Manasseh was only twelve when he became king. He was not at all a very good king. He was dreadfully wicked; he even burned and sacrificed his own sons! He also practiced sorcery and witchcraft. This went totally against the teaching of God! He led the children of Israel away from God and the teachings of the Book of I Am. The Lord spoke to Manasseh and his people, but they did not listen. He was eventually taken as a prisoner; his nose was hooked, and he was put into shackles. He was then taken away to Babylon.

Manasseh finally began to look to the Lord and pray. In his distress, he repented somewhat and tried to make some changes. Manasseh had begun to realize the importance of humbling oneself to the Lord. He attempted to turn back to God. After he died, his son, Amon, took over. He too did evil things and followed in his father's footsteps. The cycle of evil was continued! There were many very bad kings who were rebellious. Amon was Josiah's father.

They allowed idols and idol worship within the holy temple that had been dedicated solely to the Lord! There were images of the sun god Baal, carved idols and poles, and incense altars. When Josiah became king, he was appalled by this! He had the temple cleansed and purged of all the idols, and the idolatrous paraphernalia associated with them was destroyed. Josiah was the exact opposite! He made a significant difference! He did what was right in the eyes of God! He too then walked in the ways of King David. His trust led him to live for God in everything he did. He led the people back to God, and they often read the Book of I Am. His father was brutally killed by his very own officials. The legend of the young King Josiah is found in 2 Kings 21:26-23:30.

The Book of I Am is indeed fascinating! It is an extraordinary chronicle of events that took place over thousands of years. It recorded authentic reliable history. The children knew that the power was embracing all of the truth. They were taught not to compromise anything in the Book of I Am! Time after time, they had been taught and given illustrations of all the many ways the devil continued to deceive and trick the people and get them to do their own thing—to not adhere to what God had said but do as they pleased. How ludicrous it was, because they knew that the devil and his imps' job was to undermine God's authority on earth and get people to believe only part of the truth. When he could do this, he knew that he could gain a stronghold on their life and usher in much pain, turmoil, and destruction. He wanted to tear down marriages and families. He wanted to be recognized rather than for them to honor God in their lives! This was why the devil allowed them to do as they pleased rather than seek to become disciplined! This was how he gained control over their lives. The same is true today!

During this time travel journey in the Enchanting Legends, the children would again learn the benefits of being responsible and having the right priorities. Living at Shiloh Mansion was indeed interesting. The children were aware that there was a much deeper meaning to life. There was a reason why they lived the way they did. They had been raised in such a way that they were to make a positive impact on the lives of others all over the world. They were to live out the very principles that they had been taught. The very principles that their parents modeled for them. The times were rapidly changing in the world, and many still did not at all subscribe to nor believe in the Book of I Am. Many had begun to doubt and embraced alternative ways to live. Many were quite contrary to what was written in the sacred Holy Word! Some refused to acknowledge it at all. They sought to change it, water down its truth and effectiveness, and then make it genderless and not matter. So they treated the Book of I Am as though it too was perhaps just full of fairytales, or that was then and what was happening now was only what's important, so seize the moment. They did not value the ageless spiritual wisdom and knowledge that one could acquire nor realized the power and authority it had to actually change lives!

Daniel, Eliza, and Faith knew better. They realized that the Book of I Am was totally true! That there was spiritual power beyond measure like no other, and that it was actually alive! That was the miracle that made it far and above any other recorded written documents! They knew that each day was a precious gift from God! Therefore, they lived each day to grow and become all they were meant to be. They had been taught that life was not to be taken for granted, and that there was nothing more valuable than time. Their family had been gifted with many gifts; and they must strive to faithfully live according to the principles in the Book of I Am, not in a religious, legalistic way that most people thought. They actually had a lot of freedom and very liberal parents!

Many had been misled and deceived. They thought that you just went to a place where the church gathered together and that was that! You could then do whatever you wanted. Some still sincerely worshipped God and realized that you lived in the world; but yet, you lived differently. Your standards and morals came from the Book of I Am! You were considered to be peculiar for thinking that the Word actually had power! You were possibly considered abnormal or wanting to be perfect. This was why it had been abandoned by so many. The many fictitious pretended superheroes in the movies were given more credence. Therefore, many thought that it just was not possible to live your life to please God. After all, nobody was perfect and the outdated ideas and principles did not support modern day society!

However, their family was and remained dedicated to living out the way of its principles, and the children respected their parents even more for this very reason! If no one else knew, they knew what type of parents they had. They were eye witnesses to the love they shared, embraced, and demonstrated! They fully appreciated that they had been chosen to know these extremely important truths of life. This unlocked their faith; and because of this, they were able to time travel and experience the deeper, fulfilling, and rewarding purpose of life!

They knew that God's Word was real and that it was the Book of Truth! So here they were, now actually transported miraculously, back in the day when Josiah was still king. They had traveled back in time. They later discovered that at this time of their visitation, Josiah was not a little boy anymore. He was now in his early twenties. Although the children could travel in time, they couldn't change what has already been. Once they entered the travel zone, their clothing automatically changed appropriately so they could blend in somewhat. They could only observe, took in the culture, learned from what they saw firsthand, and interacted with the people. Their faith and trust had opened unimaginable insightful wisdom and was reinforced and strengthened each journey.

Once they left the people in the Enchanting Legends, the people had no recollection that the children were actually ever there. They couldn't change what had already happened. However, they must remain alert and continuously be aware since they were from the future. The imps sought to thwart their mission and kept them in undetermined limbo. Therefore, they were still subject to the present dangers, because the devil and his imps did not want them to share their faith!

The powers and principalities would have it, so they were not able to return once again to the twenty-first century. The imps were all about them in various forms. The children were in fact a threat. Just think, what would happen if everyone realized the intrinsic multiplicity of spiritual values in the Book of I Am! The devil would have far less influence and power over their lives! One should always remember "Then you will know the truth and the truth will set you free!" John 8:32 (NIV).

Lady Angelica had read to them from the Book of I Am many times the legend of Josiah. They had read it as well for themselves. They knew that Josiah was raised in one of the worst possible family environments yet, he himself managed to still honor God! Yes, he lived in a palace. But his father was not a nice man. Although Josiah was very young, he still did not act foolishly. He instead humbled himself before the Lord. There was a terrible moral decline all around him.

It is during Josiah's reign that they had learned that the prophet Jeremiah received his call from the Lord and became Josiah's advisor. It had been a long time since the people had honored God before him. Josiah knew that idolatry was wrong! Together, they encouraged the people to honor God! Josiah consistently lived for God. During his first eight years as king, he studied about God from the earliest scrolls. They were later complied into the Book of I Am. As young as sixteen, according to 2 Chronicles 34, Josiah demonstrated his commitment and dedication to God. The fabulous, magnificent temple that was dedicated to God was actually built by King Solomon. The temple had been desecrated, neglected, and in disrepair! Josiah had decided that once again the temple needed to be repaired, refurbished, cleansed, and restored!

* * *

As the children walked in anticipation along the dusty paved terrain, they were aware how very different their surroundings were from that at home. As they entered the land of the Enchanting Legends, they ended up outside of the city in the forest. As they walked along, there was no clear path. The air was much drier as well. Now as they were approaching the city of Jerusalem, they could begin to see more of a natural path coming to view. The dust had settled along the way here because of the many travelers. Ahead was a place that was much more heavily populated. In the city, many of the streets were roughly paved. However, still nothing like at Shiloh Mansion. They were no longer among the forest adjacent to their home where there was plush, immensely dense, green foliage.

It was somewhere about 665 Bc. There were no passports to check or border patrols, no airplanes or airport security. Obviously, there was no modern transportation; of course, there were no cars, taxicabs, buses, laptop computers, or smartphones or cell phones to call home. The children did see donkeys, a few horses, and lots of camels; but they themselves were traveling by foot. However, they were monitored via their invisible GPS wristbands that tracks their journey! On some of the streets, they noticed wagons; but the wheels were wooden. They also knew that God is omnipresent!

One thing that they did have was their bottomless water bottles that were automatically transformed along with their clothing. It was replenished from the unseen moisture in the air! Water always has and always will be. Past, present, and future, it is a life sustainer! The majority of the human body is made up of water! The brain itself is at least seventy percent water! Amazingly, their source of water remained endless. Their containers continuously filled up automatically with clean, fresh, filtered water. During the transition, their clothing was now woollike and not at all as vibrantly colorful. The girls now had shawls that were appropriate for the day and age. They all now of course had on leather thong sandals. How close or far from civilization they would be when they entered their time travel journey remained to be seen? It was always a mystery, because they never knew exactly just where they would end up. They arrive at some very interesting and unusual time spots at times.

"Wow! We are finally here!" the girls said again.

Here in the land of Jerusalem, they had come to meet King Josiah. By modern standards, Jerusalem was smaller than the large cities where they were from. There were no hotels. Visitors were usually few, far and in between, because of the long distance one must travel during this time period. Most of the people were residents. Yet, in Jerusalem at this time, there were many more visitors than usual than in the surrounding towns; because here was where the king resided. Judah was a monarchy, and Josiah was king. There was no such thing as church and state being separate at that time. It is so much different now! In times of yore the king or monarch had the rule over both the state as well as the church. Thomas Jefferson actually passed an amendment saying, "there is a wall of separation between church and state. Congress shall make no law respecting an establishment of religion, or prohibiting the free exercise thereof… This was actually addressed to the Danbury Baptist Association in Connecticut and published in a Massachusetts Newspaper in January of 1802. This continues to be debatable today.

As they walked along, they noticed most of the houses were designed with an upper story. They had learned during their studies that this was where the family usually sleeps. There were no beds or pretty comfy down or satin comforters or adjoining bathroom suites with running water like they have at Shiloh Mansion. Certainly no grand staircase like at Shiloh Mansion. The downstairs living area usually served as the living area during the day. At night, it's transformed for sleep; and the family curled up or slept on handwoven mats or even on the rooftop when weather's hot. They noticed that it was a lot more people about than they expected. The houses seemed overcrowded. There appeared to be masses of people everywhere.

As they continued to walk, they noticed further up ahead what must be, no doubt, the Temple Mount! It was north of the city. The temple was built on Mt. Moriah. King David had received the plans from the Lord and passed the plans on to his son Solomon (1 Chronicles 28). They could see what appeared to be a huge, massive courtyard. The temple itself was huge. Wow! It was gleaming and gigantic! It couldn't be missed since it was over twenty stories tall, covered in gold. It was centered in the middle of the courtyard. There were three tall gates about ten stories tall, each with seven steps entering into the outer courtyard. There were also three tall gates that entered into the inner court, each with eight steps. The inner courtyard was on a raised platform. There was a brass altar set squarely in the courtyard built in front of the temple door. They had learned that it took many years to build the magnificent temple! There were again many people milling about. No doubt they were preparing for some type of festivities!

Although the architecture was quite different from what they were accustomed, they saw that they must definitely be close to where Josiah lived as well. They knew that some of the architectural features that were used in building the palace were used in building the temple or the house of the Lord. It was evident that his palace too was quite majestic or even more so grand of a place. They saw it too! No one could ever really put on paper or canvas what it really looked like, as far as they knew. Remember once again, many didn't totally believe the Book of I Am, although it gave a true, thorough description of how it was built and its contents. It was hard for many to believe that way back then without all the modern tools and conveniences one could possibly build a palace so enormously grand. How could it be built, or was it really that grand? But as the children saw it, it was still beyond what they ever would have imagined! The city around it was far different in comparison. They knew that the temple had originally been built by King Solomon. Yes! This is their destination! Their wristbands were now beeping.

Although they were time travelers, the children were usually received as prophets from afar, because they had so much wisdom. Prophets were known for their wisdom and ability to foretell what was coming. They usually warned the people. So in a sense, this was a valid perception. Here in Judah, they did not know that Jesus had already been born of the Virgin Mary and lived a sinless life, was crucified, died, and was buried. Then he arose after three days with all power from the grave. This was also another reason why they were confident when on their time travel journeys. It was during this time that they really did know what the future would bring! The truth had been confirmed! They were believers!

As they walked boldly toward the palace, several of the guards approached them and asked. "Where are you going?"

"We have come to see the king."

"You have what?" And the guards began to laugh a thunderous laugh.

"You, who are but commoners, and you want to see the king?" said the guard.

"What business might you have with the king?" The guards made this assumption. By the way, they were dressed in clothing appropriate for travel. They were still in traveling clothes and were a bit dusty from walking as well!

"Yes, we would like to see the king," said Daniel confidently. "We have traveled from afar, and we are anxious to see King Josiah," said Daniel.

CHAPTER 6

"We are here on a mission to see King Josiah. We have traveled from afar," said Daniel. There was a lot going on around the temple. King Josiah had ordered that they once again observe the Passover a few years back. So there was a lot of activity going on at this time as the Passover celebration drew near. This was one of the feasts that was recorded in the Book of I Am as well. Several years back, they had discovered the actual sacred scrolls of the Book of I Am. So now, each year, Passover was again festively honored and observed. Josiah wanted to follow all of the laws from the Book of I Am. He knew that this was how he could be victorious in whatever he set out to do!

Since it was the time of Passover, the children now knew that they were in the beginning of the month of April while in the Enchanting Legends. No wonder why it was so busy! Everyone in Jerusalem took a part in the great gala, enormous festivities. Many traveled from afar. They could see and certainly smell the fragrant aroma as they were making the many burnt sacrifices. This had started in the early wee hours of the morning and would be going on through the night. This was when their history lessons and readings from the Book of I Am came in handy! They knew what the huge pots, caldrons, enormous kettles, and all the different people meant. But what was so surprising, they had not really imagined all the multitudes of animals along with the smells. They now realized that King Josiah would be quite busy, and it would be difficult to personally meet and spend time with him since so much was going on. Security was tighter about the palace as well. But at least they could see the gatekeepers assembling at the gates, and they could see and hear the singers. It was really something.

What was always a challenge was actually maneuvering among the people and learning the ways and customs of the era they visited. It was here that they learned and sharpened their people skills. Here, they had to rely on their natural spiritual gifts and talents rather than technology!

"This is really interesting, I had imagined somewhat as to what it would be like! But I had not at all imagined that it would be this busy. I see it takes a lot of preparation for Passover! The temple is magnificent, it is so huge and the palace...wow! It is just like it was described in the Book of I Am," said Eliza. "I just love all the animals, cattle, sheep, camels, and goats too; and there must be thousands of them. But I could do without the smell." Eliza and Faith both fanned their noses and laugh!

"This is one big barbeque! Although it is kind of sad that they are sacrificed and all, but I understand. Imagine those who live near the slaughter houses! Is it any different than when we are back at home? We eat beef or lamb and...we just don't see it alive before it is actually slaughtered and then cooked. Well, unless you live on a farm. Right! But, I never really, actually thought about ever eating any of the animals at the safari park," said Faith.

"The difference is when they sacrificed the animals, they are actually celebrating their freedom from when they came out of Egypt. It is a part of their traditional customs," said Daniel. "Now in the twenty-first century, we don't do that anymore. We realize that Jesus was the ultimate Lamb of God; and since he sacrificed his life for us as we learned in the Book of I Am, we don't have to make live animal sacrifices anymore! We are free!" said Daniel.

"Well, that is great!" said Eliza. "I would not like the idea of having to sacrifice the animals in the safari park or—"

"Me too!" said Faith.

Daniel just chuckled. "You two are quite the characters. Let's move a little closer to the palace."

As Daniel and the girls began to walk closer toward the palace, one of the king's men asked him. "Can I help you?"

This time with authority, Daniel told him that they were there on a mission and had come to see King Josiah. "We have journeyed from afar and have come to see the king!"

Well, it was true; but they certainly would not say from how far. Yeah! Like many years into the future. Passover was also a time for national repentance. It was to be a weeklong celebration commemorating the time when the children of Israel left Egypt after they were delivered from slavery. It was known as the exodus in the Book of I Am. Each family sacrificed a young lamb or goat, and they ate matzo (unleavened bread). This was bread basically made of flour and water and cooked very quickly.

The most important thing to remember was what Passover was really all about. How they traditionally commiserated, honored, and celebrated their freedom! There was a sense of merriment in the air. You could feel the excitement. The children were glad and really excited that they had been able to come at such a festive time as this.

The guard looked at Daniel and the girls and immediately realized that there was something very uniquely different about them. There was a sense of wisdom and authority he recognized in them. The three of them exuded something that was unexplainable, which he was not usually accustomed to.

"Wait here, I will see if I can help you." Then he disappeared momentarily.

The children continued to meander in the immediate vicinity amid all of the people. "Just think of all the cool stuff King David provided for Solomon to build the temple many years ago," said Daniel.

Daniel was quite the history buff; and he had really enjoyed the legends about David, his son Solomon, and all the kings. The idea of a king ruling a nation at eight years old was quite fascinating. It all came in handy, especially at this time.

"I think they are going to let us in!" said Faith. Up until now, Faith had been fairly quiet. She had been looking around, a bit mesmerized, and was just taking in everything. The ability to time travel was indeed different. But remember, although very smart and responsible, the children were still children.

Yes, they lived at Shiloh Mansion. But remember, the temple was twenty stories tall and was overlaid with gold. There were huge gates and so many people were going about the place. King Josiah had to do a lot of work refurbishing the temple. It had been neglected and misused. How wonderful it must be to actually see it all firsthand!

"Wow!" said Faith.

Daniel stared ahead and said, "Yes, they are going to let us in. Perhaps they have sent word to the king that we are here!"

Remember, Daniel had superabilities. He could see through walls, and they all could also soar. While on a time travel journey, this was helpful when or if it was ever necessary to escape. Remember, their special abilities were significantly enhanced when time traveling as well.

As the children continued to roam about, they nodded and smiled to the many people they encountered. Everyone seemed to be quite friendly. Ahead, they saw the guard. It appeared as though he was walking toward them. This time when he returned, he had a host of guards along with him. One spoke for them all. "We have been informed that an invitation has been extended to you. However, if the king personally acknowledges you at the festivities tonight, that will remain to be seen. But first, in any case, you must get prepared. We will take you to a place where you can get prepared and rest a bit from your travels."

Daniel nodded and said, "Point the way." Daniel winked at the girls and said, "See!"

One must remember the fact that they were invited to stay at the palace, and that was an honor in itself. But to see the king would even be a greater honor! You couldn't just come to him in any kind of way. But evidently, the way has been made; but the children had been invited to go and tidy up a bit from their long journey. Little did the guards or anyone else knew that their long journey was from far, far away in the future.

King Josiah had now reinstated what rabbis called the Mitzvah of Hakhel, which means "the command of assembly." This is found in the Book of I Am in Deut. 31

(KJV). The Passover was now once again celebrated, and every trace of all the idols and paganism had been removed from the temple and destroyed in a big bonfire in Kidron. Josiah had once again set the temple in order. It was said that, "Now, before him there was no king like him who returned to the Lord with all his heart and with all his soul. And with all his might, according to all the law of Moses, nor did any arise like him after" (2 Kings 23, (NIV)).

As they walked through the courtyard, they could see that they were preparing for what could possibly be lunch or a midafternoon meal. There were generous platters loaded with assorted breads, olives, fruits, and what smelled delicious was some type of stew. The children were not hungry, because they had just eaten. They continued to walk briskly and picked up momentum. The weather was moderate and pretty dry, not too hot or cold. The sky above was quite beautiful. It was set like a canopy flowing with colors of pink, shades of blue, grays, and white. What was amazing was that they realized that it was the same sky everywhere!

The king's palace and temple complex was quite vast. By contrast, it dominated the city of Jerusalem. It was easy to see that a lot of labor had gone into building this huge complex. It made one wonder how they could have possibly accomplished it all without all the modern technology they had in the twenty-first century. There were many, many servants all bustling hurriedly about. They could see the singers and musicians gathering to begin to rehearse for the festivities.

The *mazkir* received them, he was what we know as the herald who came and announced that they would be taken to quarters where they could bathe, relax, and prepare for the evening festivities. At this time, they would possibly meet the king. The children were excited but remained courteously calm. They would be separated; the girls would go to one place and Daniel to another, to a bathing fountain located within the palace. Here, there was a fountain in perpetual motion. It was filled with mineral water and scented oils, and the girls experienced a fragrant of flowers with petals bobbing gently in the brisk, agitated flowing waters. The air was clean and humid inside with a wonderful perfumed fragrant aroma of exotic flowers. There were attendees there to accommodate them. They could see the beautiful gardens full of lovely ornamental shrubs and flowers. Many of these were used to create the oils and perfumes used in the palace. In the far background were mountains. They could again also hear the musicians and singers preparing for the festivities. Celebration was in the gleeful, excited atmosphere!

As the girls anxiously prepared to get ready, they knew that they had in their now transformed backpacks all they would need. Their traveling satchels were automatically filled and updated with the dressy, formal, appropriate apparel for the evening. They no longer would be adorned in the neutral, dusty travel garments. The regal evening attire would be much more colorful and festive and appropriate to meet the king. That was the beauty of time traveling. They knew how to prepare for what was ahead, because it had already been. Their backpacks had been preprogrammed and contained what each of them needed for the journey! Now, they rested a bit and emerged ready and dressed appropriately to meet King Josiah. They were now reunited with Daniel who was looking quite his well-groomed self as usual! "You two look great!"

Eliza and Faith twirled around smiling with cute half curtsies saying, "Thank you, my lord!"

Everyone was always so fascinated with Daniel, because he was so well versed and arduously amicable. He always, so comfortably fitted in wherever they were. So the girls were at ease. They all had studied feverishly and were aware as much as possible of the environment that they would be in. Fortunately during this time, there were a lot of guests; therefore, there was not a lot of time to question them. There were guards plentifully stationed throughout the palace, so they were allowed to leisurely roam throughout certain sections to admire the fascinating architecture until the festivities began. They realized it would be a few minutes or a brief moment if any time at all was spent visiting with King Josiah. There was just so much going on. But it was clear that the palace was a grand place. They were not awestruck, because they lived in Shiloh Mansion, which was by all modern standards a grand place. But they were certainly impressed! They were enchantingly delighted and thrilled as well for the opportunity to be on another time travel journey into the Enchanted Legends.

Shiloh Mansion's name held a wealth of history! Shiloh the name itself was a reminder of King David's perpetual covenant with God and his descendants that would continue to hold the scepter and to sit on the throne as king of Israel. Shiloh means sanctuary or meeting place, a place of peace. Shiloh also means coming of the Messiah! The scepter that King Josiah held had first been put into the hands of King David way back in 1010 BC (see 1 Samuel 2, KJV). At this time, God promised him a perpetual dynasty. "I have made a covenant with My chosen, I have sworn to My servant David: 'Your seed I will establish forever, and build up your throne to all generations'" (Ps. 89:3–4, NIV). "His seed also I will make to endure forever, and his throne as the days of heaven" (Ps. 89:29, KJV). "Once I have sworn by my holiness; that I will not lie unto David: His seed shall endure forever, and his throne as the sun before me; it shall be established forever like the moon, and as a faithful witness in heaven" (Ps. 89:35-37, KJV).

Here again, we find as always the significant importance of their learning from the Book of I Am. It was King Solomon who had inherited the throne from his father, David. Remember, David wanted to build the temple; but since he had been a man of war, he was able to only gather all the wonderful materials for the temple, to be later built by his son Solomon. David was also known as "a man after God's own heart!" (Acts 13:22, KJV). The rest is history! There were many kings that did not honor God and the Book of I Am. But how amazing! Here the children were standing in the palace that was built by King Solomon.

"Eliza, this is so much better than any video game that we have ever played. Listen! Notice how our voices echo when we talk," said Daniel.

"I wonder if I yelled, how far you could hear it or what would happen!" said Eliza, smiling a little sheepishly. "Just kidding, but you know I won't," she said to Daniel nodding her head.

Faith had started to hum along with the singers you could hear outside. "They have wonderful acoustics here. You could really sing with ease in here, it carries your voice so effortlessly! Who would have thought that earlier today we were sitting in the gazebo of angels, and now we are finally here! Although it is summer at home, it is spring here. It really is quite fascinating," said Faith. In the background, you could hear the trumpets!

"I think it is time to…Well, it looks like it is time to join the festivities! Let's go! The guard is pointing for us to prepare to enter into the grand court," said Daniel.

The children began to assemble as all the other guests who had come from all around had also assembled. As everyone assembled, they realized just how many people were here. They had really come at a great time to see so many people. "It is so wonderful being here. You know we cannot stay forever. But it really has been quite interesting," said Daniel.

"I know. It really has been a long day for us. We probably should be getting back. I just wanted to wave anyway. I knew we would not have a sit down, how's-your-day-going kind of talk with King Josiah. It is great, the fact that they even let us in the palace. But of course, they could not resist. God opens the path and the hearts for us! Wow! That was neat being able to spend as much time here as we have," said Eliza.

"Look, he is walking our way!" said Daniel. King Josiah gallantly paused in front of them and smiled, their eyes met amid all the gazing onlookers. This in itself was a gallant gesture. Who were they that King Josiah took the time to momentarily nod to acknowledge them? He waved as he passed. It was obvious that the Lord's favor rested upon them! There was an enormous entourage all about him.

"Well, that was a treat in itself. At least we got to, well, almost meet him. Well maybe next time!" said Faith.

"We better start heading back. My wristband is gently moving. We have had a fantastically wonderful time. We really got to see a lot! The temple was incredibly fantastic! This palace is not too shabby as well," said Daniel. Eliza, Faith, and Daniel began to walk excitedly through the massive crowd.

You could smell the aroma of the pungent aromatic incenses, burning candles, and exotic foods. It was almost overpowering and also a bit intoxicating! It was unexplainable, nothing like they had ever experienced before. But who needed to explain when you could see it up close and personal. "This was so wonderful!" said Faith.

"Yes, we must come again!" said Eliza. She was putting her poised waved hand up in a regal motion jokingly.

"Come on, you two. Time to go travelers," said Daniel.

"But we didn't get our kisses," said Eliza.

"Now, I know it's time to go; you are losing it," said Daniel. The girls giggled as they strolled through the court and out to the open pavilion and journeyed toward the gates.

"This really was fun and so amazing!" said Daniel. The children picked up speed as they commenced joyously walking in a faster upbeat rhythmic cadence. Going through the town again, they could see the great differences between palace life and living in the town. The streets were still full of jovial clusters of people celebrating everywhere. The houses stacked and ever so closely clustered together with quaint narrow passageways, which were all beautifully illuminated with candles. The air was dryer there, so the flavorful smells permeated the atmosphere around the city. There were not as many beautiful, lavish, plush green trees and shrubbery that were surrounding the palace. As they walked, there were nods. The people assumed, from the way that they were dressed, that they must be very important visitors from afar. Remember, they still had on clothing fit for the king.

They favorably reflected back on the palace visit. Before the grand celebration, they were able to venture freely about and had gotten a chance to peer into the temple. It was so wonderfully magnificent! It was large and open. Outside they saw how they had prepared and were making thousands of sacrifices of lambs. The smell was so vehemently strong and again almost overpowering! The musicians were playing, and incense burned continually. By this time, it had been going on all day and would continue on throughout the night. It was at the night festivities that the priests and guest were feasting and celebrating! Passover was a time of remembering. It brought a lot of people together from all around. And yes, little did they know they had three special time travelers from the future, the twenty-first century, from Shiloh Mansion. Who would have ever thought?

The children had now left out of the city and had begun to soar high above and were entering the forest. It never took as much time to get back as it took to get to their destination. It all really happened in a matter of minutes!

"Okay, we are here," said Daniel as they gently landed on the ground. Faith took out her pouch of silver sprinkles and the portal opened as they entered and passed through then it rapidly closed. "Wow! That really was something! We are back! Look, right where we started from this morning, same clothes and everything," said Daniel as he brushed himself down. It was almost as if he needed to touch himself to see that it really had not been a dream.

"Fascinating, absolutely fascinating," said Eliza.

Faith hummed to herself and smiled, "What a way to begin summer! Guess what, we have so many more adventures to look forward to!"

CHAPTER 7

Today was the first day of summer; and by now, it was approaching the early dawn of evening. The children were ecstatically excited and gaily frolicked around in the woods a bit. They had thoroughly enjoyed themselves but were quite happy to be back! The memories of their thrilling, exhilarating, awe-inspiring adventure into the Enchanting Legends continued to linger. The tall trees kept the still hot, brisk-glistening sunlight off them as it peered through the tall, lush green foliage. The trees provided a consoling, comforting shade. The fresh, unsullied, clean smell of being close to home was quite delightful.

"Smell that! Now that is what I call good fresh air. Not that it smelled bad at all, along with all the incense. It just had a unique overpowering, aromatic pungent barbeque kind of smell mingled together all at once. I sure hope we are not having lamb for dinner tonight! Because if we are,

I am going to ask Cook to prepare me something else!" said Daniel.

"I am with you on that! No lamb for me either," said Eliza.

"No beef for me," said Faith. They had now begun the walk back to Shiloh Mansion. They still had plenty of time to prepare for dinner at seven!

BIBLIOGRAPHY

Note: You may use the link below for easy and fast way of citing copyrighted materials: http://citationmachine.net/index2.php?reqstyleid=10&mode=form&rsid=1&reqsrcid=ChicagoBook&more=yes&nameCnt=1

Cover Photo
  Beach Forest in Denmark by Malene Thyssen
  Wikipedia.org free images
  Public Domain
  http://en.wikipedia.org/wiki/File:Grib_skov.jpg

Research From

Barnes Notes by Baker*Barnes Notes*. Grand Rapids Michigan: Baker Book House Company, 1987.

Matthew Henry Commentary On the Whole Bible by Hendrickson Publishers Inc, Peabody Massachusetts, 1992